GREEK BEASTS AND HEROES

The Dragon's Teeth

You can read the stories in the
Greek Beasts and Heroes series in any order.

If you'd like to read more about some
of the characters in this book, turn to pages
76–78 to find out which other books to try.

Atticus's journey continues
on from *The Harp of Death*.

To find out where he goes next,
read *The Hero's Spear*

Turn to page 79 for a complete list
of titles in the series.

...ND HEROES

The Dragon's Teeth

LUCY COATS

Illustrated by Anthony Lewis

Orion
Children's Books

Text and illustrations first appeared in
Atticus the Storyteller's 100 Greek Myths
First published in Great Britain in 2002
by Orion Children's Books
This edition published in Great Britain in 2010
by Orion Children's Books
a division of the Orion Publishing Group Ltd
Orion House
5 Upper St Martin's Lane
London WC2H 9EA
An Hachette UK company

1 3 5 7 9 8 6 4 2

A catalogue record for this book is available from the British Library

ISBN 978 1 4440 0073 3

Printed in China

www.orionbooks.co.uk
www.lucycoats.com

For Jon Appleton, excellent editor,
with love and thanks.
L. C.

For Nana
A. L.

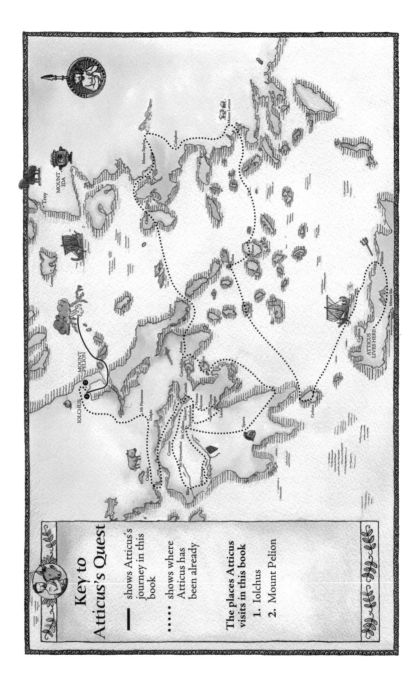

Key to Atticus's Quest

—— shows Atticus's journey in this book

······ shows where Atticus has been already

The places Atticus visits in this book
1. Iolchus
2. Mount Pelion

Contents

Stories from the Heavens

Long ago, in ancient Greece, gods and goddesses, heroes and heroines lived together with fearful monsters and every kind of fabulous beast that ever flew, or walked or swam. But little by little, as people began to build more villages and towns and cities, the gods and monsters disappeared into the secret places of the world and the heavens, so that they could have some peace.

 9

Before they disappeared, the gods and goddesses gave the gift of storytelling to men and women, so that  nobody would ever forget them. They ordered that there should be a great storytelling festival once every seven years on the slopes of Mount Ida, near Troy, and that tellers of tales should come from all over Greece and from lands near and far to take part. Every

seven years a beautiful painted vase, filled to the brim with gold, magically appeared as a first prize, and the winner was honoured for the rest of his life by all the people of Greece.

 10

Atticus hobbled along on a stick. "We shan't get to Troy at all at this rate," he grumbled, looking at his swollen toe. "I wish I could get this thorn out. I shall have to ask for a healer in the next village."

The healer tied the linen bandage off neatly. "It shouldn't give you any more trouble now," she said.

Atticus fumbled in his wallet to pay her, but she shook her head.

"You're a storyteller. You can pay me with a story while you rest that foot a bit."

The Centaur Healer

The goatherd called and whistled to his dog, but she took no notice, so he went to find her.

She was lying on the ground together with his best nanny goat, and between their front legs was a baby boy, whom they were licking tenderly.

The goatherd stooped to pick the boy up, but suddenly a bright light shone round him. The goatherd scratched his head. "Must be the child of a god," he thought. "Better leave it alone."

Later that day the baby, whose name was Asclepius, snuggled sleepily into his father Apollo's cloak as he flew towards

 12

the centaur Chiron's cave on Mount
Pelion. Chiron was the greatest teacher
and healer of all time, and kings and
princes were sent to him to learn how to
be heroes.

Asclepius became Chiron's star pupil.
He was eager to learn everything his
master could teach, and soon he knew
the use of every healing herb on earth as

well as the meaning of every star in the sky. And what he didn't learn from Chiron, he learnt from his father, Apollo, who visited him often.

When he grew up, he went to his master and knelt before him.

 14

"Dear Chiron," he said. "I need to go out into the world. I want to help the people of Greece, and I want to teach others to heal."

Chiron patted his head and gave him his blessing.

Asclepius soon had queues of sick people outside his little house. People on stretchers, people on crutches, people with cuts and fevers – everyone who came was treated, and they all left dancing and singing the praises of Asclepius the great doctor.

They liked him so much that they built temples in his honour, and Asclepius put beds in them, so that people could stay there and recover from their illnesses.

Asclepius had a tall staff, all twined round with living snakes, and as he went

round the beds, he listened to the snakes,
who told him many secrets about how to
cure people.

In time, he married, and he had seven
children, all of whom he taught to be
doctors too.

His daughter, Hygeia, was very good
at keeping people clean, and all her
patients were scrubbed and healthy in
no time at all.

Apollo was very proud of his son, and he persuaded the goddess Athene to give Asclepius two jars of the Gorgon Medusa's blood.

The one from the right side of her body was used for bringing the dead back to life, and the one from the left could be used to kill.

Asclepius never used the second, but he used the first one a great deal, and it was this that got him into trouble.

Both the Fates and Hades complained to Zeus that their work was being interfered with, but Apollo showed Zeus how healthy everyone now was, and how much good his son was doing.

"I'll let him off this time," said Zeus. "But he mustn't use it again."

One day,
Asclepius was
approached by a
man whose only
son had died.
"Please, please,
please help him,"
wailed the man.
"He's only seven!
I'll give you
anything!"

Now Asclepius felt so sorry for the
man that he brought the boy back to life
with the forbidden Gorgon's blood.

The man was so grateful he gave
Asclepius bags and bags of gold. But
when Zeus found out he was furious,
and he threw a thunderbolt which killed
not only the man and his son, but
Asclepius too.

When Apollo saw the grey ashes that had been his son blowing about in the breeze, he was determined to have his revenge on Zeus. But Zeus was sorry for what he had done, and brought Asclepius back to life, later setting him and his serpents among the stars to shine his healing wisdom down on all doctors everywhere.

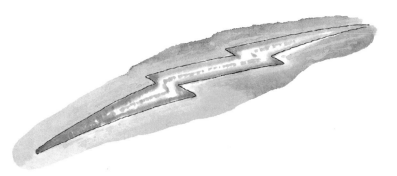

A wedding party danced up the road by the river, throwing flowers and garlands in front of the bride and groom.

"That reminds me of another wedding," said Atticus to Melissa as they passed. "Let's sit down and let them go by while I tell you the story."

The Goddesses' Quarrel

Prince Peleus was one of the pupils of Chiron the centaur. He was a great hunter and athlete, and a great favourite of the gods, too.

"I think he deserves a nice wife," said Zeus to Hera one day, and Hera agreed.

"Perhaps he'd like Thetis the nymph, although I'm not sure she wants to marry a mortal," said Hera.

"Well, if he can catch her, he can have her," answered Zeus, and he flew straight down to Chiron's cave to give Peleus the good news.

Peleus set out for the sea shore at once, and rowed himself to the tiny island

where Thetis had gone to bathe, riding on the back of her pet dolphin.

She was just taking a little nap on a bed of seaweed when Peleus grabbed her. She was so startled that she changed into a candle-flame, a jug of water, a lion and a snake, one after the other. Then she turned into a horrid slimy cuttlefish and squirted oily black ink at her husband to be, covering him from head to toe.

But Peleus never let go once, and when Thetis had calmed down, she agreed to marry him.

Hera sent her messenger Iris to everyone she could think of, inviting them all to the wedding outside Chiron's cave.

When the day came, the gods and goddesses sat on silver thrones, Hera herself lit the wedding fire, and Zeus gave the bride away.

The Muses sang, and the nereids danced, and the endless stream of wonderful presents was displayed on the white white sand.

There was a magic spear, and a golden suit of armour, a pair of immortal horses, and a magnificent chariot, as well as many other useful things for the young couple.

But Hera had forgotten to invite one person to the wedding.

23

Eris, the spirit of strife, crouched behind a bush, muttering and moaning to herself as she watched the festivities.

"I'll teach them to be happy," she snarled, as she rolled one of her golden apples towards Peleus, who was talking to Hera, Aphrodite and Athene.

As he noticed it, he picked it up, and read the writing on it out loud.

"To the Fairest," he said, puzzled. "Now who can this be for?"

Hera, Aphrodite and Athene all rushed at him.

"It's mine!" shouted Hera, grabbing at it.

"No, mine!" yelled Aphrodite, pushing her away.

"Get off, it's mine!" screamed Athene, stepping on Aphrodite's toes.

 25

The three goddesses quarrelled so much that the whole wedding was spoiled, and they flew back to Olympus, where they argued about who should have it for three whole months.

Eris was delighted. "If one little apple can do that, just think what a whole treeful could do!" she said to herself, chuckling evilly.

And off she went to plant some special quick-growing apple seeds in her gloomy garden.

Atticus had met the shepherdess just as he and Melissa had got to the bottom of Mount Pelion.

"That's Chiron's cave," she told him, as they scrambled up together beside a tumbling stream. "You can still see some writing in there."

"I'm puffed out," said Atticus, when he'd had a look. "Why don't we sit on this big stone while I tell you a story? What would you like?"

"A story about Achilles," she said. "He's my favourite hero."

The Boy in the Fire

King Peleus and Thetis the nymph had seven fine sons together, but Thetis was not happy.

"I never really wanted to marry a mortal," she grumbled as each child was born. "It's not fair that my children can't live for ever like me."

And so when each child was three days old, she hung him over a sacred fire and tried to burn away his mortal parts, afterwards rubbing him with ambrosia so that he could go and live on Olympus with the gods.

Peleus was very sad at losing his sons like this, so when the seventh child was

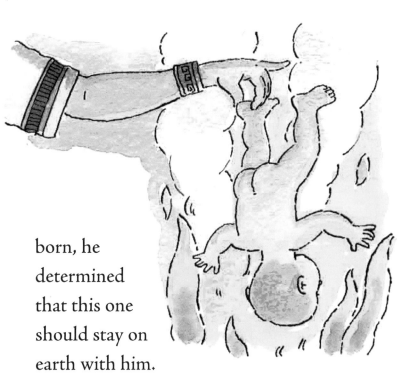

born, he
determined
that this one
should stay on
earth with him.

As Thetis turned the boy this way
and that over the sacred fire, holding him
up by one heel, Peleus rushed in and
snatched him.

"How dare you," cried Thetis, slapping
him hard, and she was so angry that she
rushed out of the palace and returned to
the sea where she had been born, and
never came back to her husband.

 29

Peleus took the crying baby and soothed him. He was now immortal, all except for the ankle and the back of the heel where his mother had been holding him. This bit was all burnt and red looking, so Peleus made his son a brand-new ankle and heel from the bones of a giant.

Peleus named his seventh son Achilles, and when he was old enough, he sent him away to be trained by Chiron the wise centaur, as Peleus had been himself.

Achilles went on to be the greatest hero ever born – but in the end his mortal heel was the cause of his death in the great war of Troy.

Atticus and Melissa had walked into the bustling city of Iolcus that morning.

"Troy's getting closer!" he thought excitedly. Wagonloads of vegetables and grain blocked the narrow streets, and they had to fight their way through to the harbour.

Suddenly, Atticus heard someone shouting his name. It was Captain Nikos.

Atticus was thankful to see him.
Getting a ship from Iolcus wasn't easy,
he'd heard.

"Do you think you could help me
find a ship to Troy?" he asked hopefully.

"Nothing easier," said Nikos. "I'm
going there myself tomorrow. You and
Melissa can come with us. Come and
meet the crew and tell us a story."

The Ship of Heroes

King Pelias of Iolcus had a nephew called Jason, a strong, handsome young man who had been hidden in Chiron's cave since he was a child to keep him safe from his enemies. He was the true heir to the throne of Iolcus, and one day he decided to go and take his kingdom back from his wicked uncle. As he walked down the slopes of the mountain, he came to a river, where an old woman stood looking feebly at the foaming waters.

"Can I help you across, my lady?" he said politely.

The old woman jumped on to his back without a word, and they set off.

As Jason got further and further into the middle of the river, the old woman seemed to get heavier and heavier, until he was sinking into the mud at every step.

As he struggled to reach the other side the sticky mud sucked one of his sandals off, and it was lost for ever.

Jason set the old lady down on the bank, and as he did so he gasped. There in front of his eyes was the goddess Hera, revealed in all her glory.

"You are a good boy to carry such a heavy load without complaining," she said. "I shall certainly help you to get your throne back."

And she disappeared.

Jason limped into the palace, one sandal on and one sandal off.

 34

 35

His Uncle Pelias noticed him at once and turned pale with horror. An oracle had once told him that a boy with one sandal would overthrow him, so he knew just who Jason was.

However, he smiled sweetly and embraced his nephew, shouting orders for a great feast to be prepared.

"Now, dear boy," he said. "You must certainly have your throne back, for I have reigned long enough. But first you must do a heroic deed to prove that you can be a good king to our people."

Then he told Jason that he must go and fetch the magical golden fleece from the land of Colchis.

"When the fleece hangs in the throne room of Iolcus, then the crown will be yours," he said.

What Pelias didn't say was that the

fleece was guarded by a fierce dragon
which never slept.

Jason gathered together all
his old school friends, and
together they built a wonderful
ship which they called the *Argo*,
with seeing eyes in the prow
and fifty oars.

 37

Before they set off they gave sacrifices to all the gods and goddesses, making sure that no one was left out or offended, and when the *Argo* sailed, she was full of fifty heroes, all ready for any kind of adventure. Heracles was there, with his friends Admetus and Hylas. Atalanta the huntress came, and so did Orpheus the poet and Castor and Polydeuces, the sons of Leda and Zeus.

They called themselves the Argonauts, and Jason was their leader and captain.

The Argonauts sailed east, on and on, until they landed in a strange country to ask the way.

All the people there were smiling and contented, except for the king, who was so thin and bony that he looked as if he might fall apart at any moment.

 38

"Whatever is the matter?" asked Jason.

The king explained that every night and morning he tried to eat, but as soon as the food was set on the table three revolting fat bird-women flew down and ate what was on his plate.

"They call themselves Harpies, and whatever they don't eat they sit in and make a mess of, so that it can't be touched," he whispered weakly. "None of my people can get rid of them, and believe me, we've tried!"

Jason and the Argonauts were hungry themselves, so they told the king to lay on a feast for that night.

 39

As soon as the disgusting Harpies swooped into the room, Calaïs and Zetes, the sons of the North Wind, flew into the air with swords and sticks and chased and whipped the Harpies until they screamed and begged for their lives.

The Argonauts laughed and cheered as they sat down to their dinner, and the king laughed with them as he stuffed food into his poor starved stomach.

The Harpies never came back, and the Argonauts got back into the *Argo* and sailed on towards Colchis.

The king had warned them about the dangerous clashing rocks they would come to on the way, and told them how to avoid them.

"If you can row as fast as a racing pigeon can fly, then you will get through," he said. "Send a bird flying ahead of your ship and you will see."

The magic rocks ground and crashed together as the Argonauts rowed near, and they were all very frightened.

Jason sent his pigeon on ahead at once, and it flew through the rocks like an arrow, coming out safe on the other side.

"Now row! Row for your lives," cried Jason, and Orpheus played a tune that made them pull with the strength of twenty men at each oar, while the goddess Hera pushed from behind.

The *Argo* whizzed past the rocks with nothing to spare, and then they were through. The rocks settled into a calm sea, and never moved again. The Argonauts had broken their spell for ever.

Although Hera helped Jason and his friends as much as she dared, there were many many more exciting adventures on their journey before they arrived safely in the city of Colchis, and set out to look for the golden fleece at last.

 44

As Atticus stopped, the sailors all groaned. "You can't leave it there!" they said.

"Come on, boys!" said Captain Nikos. "There's work to be done. Let's load the ship, and then when we've finished, Atticus will tell us how Jason got the golden fleece.

If you all work like those heroes on Argo it shouldn't take long."

Melissa trotted up the gangplank to her usual place, and soon everything was stowed. One by one the sailors sneaked up to Atticus and sat down. When Captain Nikos came aboard, he laughed.

"One more story for luck," he said. "Then I expect those sails ready in double quick time! We're catching the early tide."

The Impossible Task

The King of Colchis hated strangers. He hated them so much that he killed any who came to his country. But when he heard that Jason and his band of Argonauts had landed on his shores in search of the precious golden fleece, he smiled nastily.

"I shall set this great hero an impossible task, and then I shall kill him and his followers," he said to his witch-daughter Medea.

So the king welcomed Jason and his friends, but when they told him what they had come for he pretended to be surprised.

"Don't you know that anyone who wants

 46

the golden fleece must do something for me first? I have a field that needs ploughing up and sowing – perhaps you could do that?"

Jason agreed, but he was very surprised when he saw the king's plough animals, and even more surprised when he saw what he had to sow.

The plough was harnessed to two fiery bulls, whose breath burned anyone who came near them, and the seeds in the packet were dragon's teeth.

"You have till sunset tomorrow," said the king.

Now Hera knew that Jason could never plough and sow the field on his own, so she summoned Aphrodite.

"Make the king's daughter, Medea, fall in love with Jason," she commanded. "She will know how to help him."

So Aphrodite sent her son Eros to shoot Medea with his little love darts, and soon afterwards Medea sneaked into Jason's room.

"I love you," she whispered," and I can help you. Take this lotion and cover yourself with it. Then you will be able to bear the heat of the bulls' breath and plough the field."

Jason did just as she said, and then he sowed the dragon's teeth.

Straightaway hundreds of stone soldiers sprang up in neat rows from the ground, but Jason threw a rock at them, and they all began to fight each other. By sunset they were all dead.

The king was furious, and he ordered his soldiers to kill Jason and his Argonauts at dawn.

But Medea overheard his plan and ran to Jason at once. "You must leave," she said. "I will lead you to the sacred grove, and sing the dragon to sleep with my magic while you steal the golden fleece. Then we can escape together."

Jason kissed her, and together they tiptoed out of the palace.

The grove was dark and gloomy, but the golden fleece shone out like a thousand suns.

 50

Quickly Medea began to chant a magic song, and the green scaly dragon which had been set to guard the fleece closed its huge eyes with a sigh.

Jason stepped over its gigantic body and ripped the precious fleece from the branch where it hung.

A hundred warning bells rang out as Jason and Medea ran for the *Argo* and they heard the thunder of many

feet behind them as the king's soldiers gave chase.

They flung themselves onto the deck, and the Argonauts rowed and rowed and rowed until Colchis was left far behind.

The golden fleece was rescued at last, and Jason could now go home to Iolcus and claim his throne from his wicked uncle Pelias.

The ship slipped out of harbour in the early morning mist. The crew were all busy with the sails, so Atticus went to sit by Melissa.

"Last leg of the voyage, Melissa," he said. "Just think! All these months of travelling and we shall soon be in sight of Troy. It's a shame we don't have time to go through Thrace, and it's a pity we can't see the red anemones in flower on the mountains – but I'll tell you the story of how they got there. That'll have to do instead."

The Boy Whom Love Forgot

The myrrh tree stood waving and sighing in the breeze, the two halves of its trunk split down the middle. At its roots lay a beautiful newborn baby, gurgling and cooing as he waved his tiny fists in the air.

"What shall I do with you, my little Adonis?" said the goddess Aphrodite, as she stood looking down at him. "I'm sorry I turned your mother into a tree, but she really did annoy me. Ah well, I suppose I shall just have to look after you myself!"

Now Aphrodite was really not very good at looking after babies, so she bundled Adonis into a nice cosy chest and took him down to Tartarus.

"There's a little secret of mine in here, Persephone," she said to the queen of the Underworld. "Keep it safe for me and I'll come back for it sometime."

Persephone agreed, and she put the chest in a dark corner and completely forgot about it while she went up to the earth above to visit her mother, the goddess Demeter.

But one day, soon after her return to Tartarus she was passing the chest and it gave a cry.

"Whatever is that?" said Persephone, and she opened the lid.

What a surprise she got when she saw a lovely little boy smiling up at her. She lifted him out at once and took him to her own palace, where she petted him and spoiled him and gave him everything he wanted.

"How could Aphrodite leave you in a chest, my treasure?" she crooned. "Persephone will look after you now, my darling."

Now Aphrodite had forgotten all about Adonis, and she didn't remember until many years later when she saw Persephone again, smiling as she talked to a tall handsome youth.

"Who on earth is that gorgeous boy?" said Aphrodite, who had quite fallen in love with him.

Persephone laughed. "Why, that's your little secret that you left with me so many years ago!"

Aphrodite was furious. "How dare you steal him," she hissed, and soon the two goddesses were fighting as to who should have Adonis.

The fight went on for so long that finally Zeus himself came down to settle it.

"The boy shall live four months with each of you, and have four months on his own," he boomed.

But Aphrodite was determined to have Adonis all to herself. She put on her magic girdle and dazzled Adonis with her beauty, so that when it was Persephone's turn to have him, he wouldn't leave.

"The Underworld is so dark," he complained. "And you are so beautiful. Let me stay with you a little longer."

Aphrodite smiled a secret smile as she agreed.

Persephone waited and waited for Adonis to come, and when he didn't arrive she went to look for him.

She found him curled up asleep at Aphrodite's feet.

"Looking for someone?" asked Aphrodite sweetly.

Persephone flounced out in a rage, and went straight to Ares, who agreed to help her to get her revenge.

As Adonis and Aphrodite were out hunting on Mount Lebanon the next day, a huge white boar charged out of the bushes and rushed at Adonis.

Before Aphrodite could even scream a warning, Adonis had been gored to death by its sharp tusks.

Wherever his blood fell on the earth, small red flowers appeared, and Aphrodite made them into garlands for her hair, so that she should always remember her beloved Adonis.

As they sat there the ship's mate, a rough-looking man with a villainous scar on his cheek, came rolling across the deck.

"Captain Nikos and the boys in the crew are asking if you'd tell us a story. The wind's set fair, and the ship'll sail herself for a while."

"I've got just the one," said Atticus, and soon the sailors were listening to the story of Paris and Oenone.

The Nymph
and the Cowherd

The nymph Oenone sat on the edge of her fountain, spinning the pretty drops into a necklace as she sang to herself. It was no wonder that Paris the cowherd fell in love with her as soon as he saw her.

When Oenone looked up and saw his handsome face staring at her from behind a tree she giggled shyly and dived back into the tinkling waters.

But soon Paris had coaxed her out, and day after day they would sit together, holding hands and gazing into each other's eyes.

Paris thought that Oenone was the most beautiful name in the world, and soon he had carved it onto the trunks of all the trees in the wood.

Paris was tall and strong and his eyes were as brown as new hazelnuts.

"I don't believe you're a cowherd at all," said Oenone. "I think you must be a king's son in disguise."

And she was right, Paris was the son of Priam, the king of Troy.

Agelaus, the king's chief herdsman, had been told to kill him when he was just a baby because of a prophecy that he would one day destroy his father's city.

But Agelaus couldn't bring himself to do something so horrible, and so he had brought Paris up with his own son in secret.

When Paris grew up, he was put in charge of the king's best herd bulls, and his favourite game was to set them fighting with bulls from other herds.

"My bulls are always best," he boasted as he crowned the winner with flowers, and gave the loser an old straw hat to wear on his horns.

Soon his bulls were winning all the time, and he decided to offer a golden crown to any bull which could beat the champion of them all.

Now the gods had been listening to Paris' boasting, and they decided to challenge him themselves.

They came down and hid among the trees, and then sent Ares, disguised as a fierce black bull, to compete against Paris' champion. The fight went on for hours, but then Paris' bull began to tire.

"The golden crown is yours, oh great black bull," cried Paris at last. "You have beaten us fair and square."

And all the gods came out to congratulate him on his decision.

But Oenone sat weeping by her fountain, because she had seen in a dream that the gods would take Paris away from her, and that their happy life together in the woods would never be the same again.

"That Paris," said the ship's mate. "Wasn't he the one who caused all the trouble at Troy?"

Atticus nodded. "It was more than a bit of trouble," he said. "The Trojan War lasted for ten years, and all because the gods chose the wrong man to make an important decision. Listen, and I'll tell you the story."

The Fairest Goddess

After the wedding of King Peleus and Thetis the nymph, the gods and goddesses all went back to Olympus.

But Olympus was no longer the happy place it had once been, because Hera, Athene and Aphrodite never stopped fighting and arguing over who should own the golden apple which was labelled "To the Fairest".

They screeched and squawked and scratched like battling cats until everyone had to stick their fingers in their ears to shut out the horrible noise.

Finally Zeus and the other gods decided that someone would have to judge between

 68

them. None of the gods dared to do it, so they chose a young cowherd, Paris, the son of King Priam of Troy.

The gods liked Paris. He was good-looking and brave, and he seemed to be fair-minded and honest. So Zeus sent Hermes to fetch him to a meadow on Mount Ida, near Troy.

Paris couldn't help being a little nervous. The three goddesses were lined up in a row, each dressed in her best robes and her finest jewellery.

"They're all so beautiful," he whispered. "Maybe I should just divide the apple into three."

But Hermes shook his head. "Zeus himself has commanded you to make this

 69

choice," he said sternly. "And I really don't think you want to disobey him."

Paris sighed unhappily and walked across the meadow, the golden apple in his hand.

"Now, dear goddesses," said Paris. "You each have five minutes to tell me why you are more beautiful than your friends. When you have all finished, then I shall decide between you."

Hera immediately stepped forward and took Paris by the arm.

"Dearest boy," she said. "Surely you can see that the prize should go to me. After all, Zeus himself did choose me over all the others. And besides, if you choose me, I shall make you the most powerful king in the world. Just imagine. . . palaces full of gold, countries to rule. Everyone would have to do as you ordered. Surely you can see that the apple belongs to me."

Paris scratched his head. He was very good at herding his bulls around, but he wasn't sure he wanted to be in charge of lots of countries. It sounded like too much hard work.

"Next, please," he said, as Hera went back to her place.

Then Athene walked across the grass, and clapped an arm around his shoulders. Paris nearly fell over.

"Only the most beautiful woman in the world could have armies falling at her feet," she said. "And if you choose me, you shall command them all. You shall be my best general, and I shall make you a famous hero. Give me the apple and you shall have the strength of twenty men and the courage of a hundred lions.

No spear or sword shall ever wound you, and your shield shall turn any arrows back on those who fire them."

Paris rubbed his nose thoughtfully. Battles were noisy, and he didn't like blood much, although being that strong was quite tempting.

"Next, please," he called, as Athene strode back to her place in the line.

Only Aphrodite was left, and as she glided across the grass towards Paris she secretly slipped on her magic girdle.

"Dearest Paris," she purred. "Who else but the goddess of love could be the most beautiful woman ever?"

Paris nodded dumbly as Aphrodite put her arm around his shoulders. She smelled deliciously of summer roses and dew.

"You don't need kingdoms or armies, but what you do need is a bride almost as beautiful as me. If you give me the apple, I will let you marry Helen of Sparta, who is the loveliest mortal woman on earth."

Now Aphrodite knew perfectly well that Helen was already happily married to King Menelaus of Sparta – in fact it was she who had made Helen fall in love with him – but she didn't care one little bit. She wanted that apple so badly that she would have done anything to get it.

Paris beamed at her. The most beautiful woman in the world – that sounded just what he wanted most. He forgot all about his love for the nymph Oenone, as he fell on his knees before Aphrodite.

"The apple is yours, oh fairest of all goddesses," he croaked.

There was a whisk of cloaks and a stamp of feet as Hera and Athene stormed off in a jealous rage to plot and plan their revenge against him. But Aphrodite just smiled a secret smile of triumph as she raised Paris to his feet.

"Let's go and plan a wonderful wedding for you, my dear," she said.

Greek Beasts and Heroes and where to find them ...

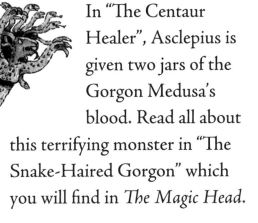

In "The Centaur Healer", Asclepius is given two jars of the Gorgon Medusa's blood. Read all about this terrifying monster in "The Snake-Haired Gorgon" which you will find in *The Magic Head*.

Both gods and humans are always being turned into things in the Greek myths – one minute a girl, the next a tree! The **Greek Beasts and Heroes** books are filled with lots of brilliant transformation stories. So why not read about poor, scared Daphne in "The Girl Who Turned into a Bay Tree" or boastful Arachne in "The Web Spinner" or clever Metis in "The Bee of Wisdom". (These stories are all in *The Monster in the Maze*.)

Would you like to read some more about the Muses? They have a story to themselves in *The Harp of Death* entitled "The Boastful Singer".

 Was Achilles *really* the greatest hero ever born? Or was he just a sulky soldier? Read more about him and decide for yourself. Don't miss "The Hero's Spear" in the book with that title.

The *Argo* set sail filled with heroes – and you can read about many of them in other **Greek Beasts and Heroes** stories. Heracles' adventures are in *The Flying Horse* and *The Harp of Death*.

Meet Atalanta in "The Brave Huntress", and read the story of Orpheus in "The Sweetest Music". Both of these stories are in *The Harp of Death*.

The tales of Troy are some of the most exciting ever told. Meet Priam and Paris again in "The Cunning Plan", which Atticus tells in *The Hero's Spear*.

Greek Beasts and Heroes
Collect them all!